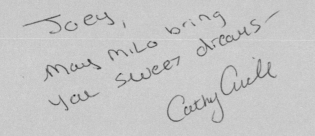

Joey,
May Milo bring
you sweet dreams—
Cathy Guill

Milo

and The Missing Wand

Making Bedtime Magical

Muffy Clarkson, Cathy Circle, & Jill Novak

With Illustrations by Brian Killeen

NK Publications
P.O. Box 1735
Radio City Station
New York, N.Y. 10101-1735
www.nkpublications.com

ISBN: 978-0-9705100-8-2

This book is dedicated with love to our own little Milos - Lexi, Matt, Connor, Matthew, Josh, and Oliver.

Meet Milo and Alacazam

The character of Milo was dreamt up by us,
three moms who wanted to create
a bedtime ritual that brings a child's day
to a close in a positive and empowering way.

Milo faces all of the ups and downs
of being a kid—but with the help of his wand,
a little bit of imagination, and a 'magical' chant,
Milo makes it easy to feel relaxed, calm,
and ready for bed. As Milo would say,
"good night everyone".

Milo likes to relax just before bed,
in his favorite pajamas –
blue, green and red.
"They are all that he'll wear,"
his mother said.

His mother, you see,
was going out for the night.
And wanted the sitter
to get everything right.

"Now Milo, be a good boy and do as you're told. You mustn't give Lucy a reason to scold."

"I've left instructions there by the phone. And before you know it, I'm going to be home."

"I'll be a good boy, I always am. But you know I can't sleep without Alacazam."

Alacazam
is a magical wand
that Milo found
catching frogs in the pond.

You see, Alacazam
is more than a friend,
it's full of spells
from end to end.

Whenever anything goes
wrong in some way,

Alacazam makes it
all seem okay.

Then just before bed,
Milo had a great fright.
"I should never have let
that wand out of my sight!"

"If I can't find it,
I won't go to bed.
I will not behave
and
my face will turn red."

So on hands and knees
they started to look.

Under the bed.
Inside a book.

But hard as they tried, it was not there.
Not in the garbage, or in Lucy's hair.

As Milo sadly climbed into bed,
he felt something lumpy
under his head.
And there was his wand
with a note from his mother.

"Good night.
Sleep tight.
Now under
the covers."

So just before Lucy turned out the light,
Milo said a chant to make everything right.

"Alacazam, Alacazam, you do magic like no one can.
Keep me safe all through the night,
dreaming dreams of pure delight.
Don't wake me up until the sun shines bright."

everyone

MiLo

Making Bedtime Magical